To Angela –
Happy reading & harmonica
playing. Hope the magic of
the harmonica comes your way...
All the best 😊
Rob Dubreuil
Dec. 2010

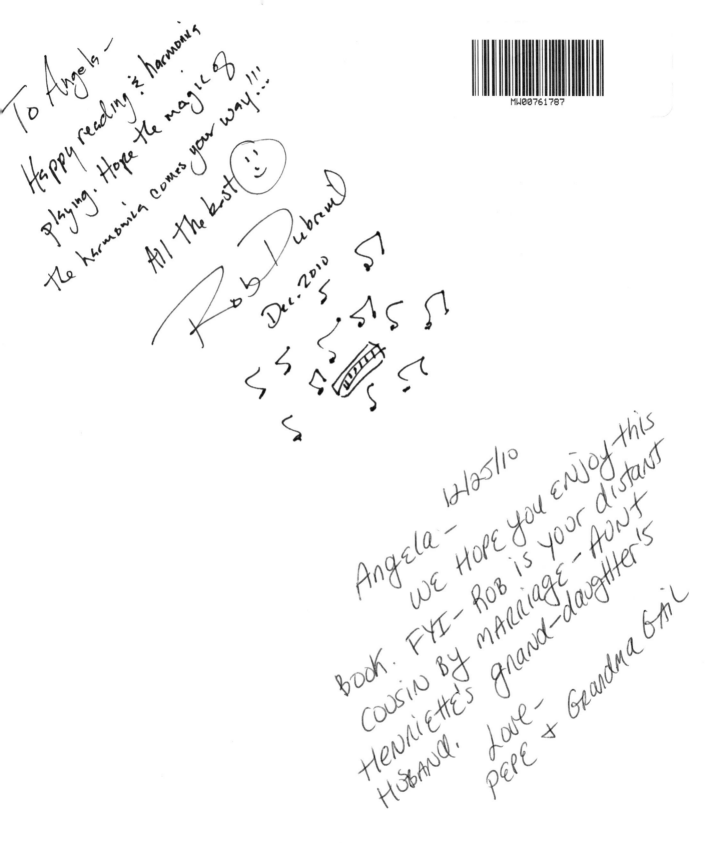

Angela – 12/25/10
We hope you enjoy this
book. FYI - Rob is your distant
cousin by marriage - Aunt
Henriette's grand-daughter's
husband. Love –
Pepe & Grandma Gail

MW00761787

Daniel and the Harmonica

By Rob Dubreuil

Illustrated by Ginger Nielson

Stemmer
House
Publishers

Inquiries should be directed to:
Stemmer House Publishers
4 White Brook Road
P.O. Box 89
Gilsum, NH 03448
www.stemmer.com

Printed and bound in the United States
First Edition, 2010

Library of Congress Cataloging-in-Publication Data

Dubreuil, Robert, 1975–
Daniel and the harmonica / by Robert Dubreuil ; illustrated by Ginger Nielson. — 1st ed.
p. cm.
Summary: Delighted with the harmonica he receives as a birthday present from his grandfather, Daniel, after much practice, plays it in the park and discovers the true magic of his grandfather's gift.
[1. Harmonica—Fiction. 2. Gifts—Fiction. 3. Music—Fiction.] I. Nielson, Ginger, ill. II. Title.
PZ7.D8547Dan   2010
[Fic]—dc22   2010022464

ISBN: 9780880450881

Daniel's birthday had finally come. He awoke earlier than normal and after his dad helped with a quick morning bath, he was dressed and running down the stairs. As he rounded the corner into the kitchen, he could smell his mother's delicious cooking.

The house was soon filled with old men, talking women, and giggling children. Daniel's grandfather reached out to give him a great, big hug. "I have a very special gift for you today, my boy," his grandfather said. Daniel could only guess at what it might be.

Everyone sang "Happy Birthday" as loud as their voices could go. In one long breath, Daniel blew out all of the candles on his cake. He opened his presents and then hugged, kissed, and thanked his whole family.

Amid all of the laughter and joy, Daniel's grandfather raised his voice to announce that there was one more gift left for Daniel. He reached into his pocket and handed the boy a small, wooden box. Inside was a harmonica.

Out of the box and now in his hands, the new harmonica shimmered like a silver bar. It was as if he was holding a point of light from the night sky above. He looked it all over, flipping it around and around. It fit perfectly into Daniel's hands.

"I used to have one when I was your age and loved it. Haven't played for a very long time, though," his grandfather said. Inside the harmonica box were lessons for songs like "I've Been Working on the Railroad" and "Red River Valley."

"You know, harmonicas are unique because you can keep them in your pocket and play them anytime. You can't do that with a tuba or piano, of course," he said with a light chuckle. "You'd be surprised how many people play the harmonica, or the harp, as some folks call it. You wait and see."

"Thank you, grandpa, I just love it," Daniel said. He marveled at the bright glow of the harmonica in the light of the parlor.

"Well, go ahead, play something," his grandfather said.

Daniel brought the instrument to his lips and blew out softly. The most beautiful sound came out. It was warm, low, and vibrating, like many voices humming together. Daniel was instantly hooked on the harmonica.

"Do you know what they say about the harmonica?" the old man whispered.

"No, grandpa."

"I've always heard that when you receive a harmonica as a gift from someone who loves you, it becomes extra special. When you learn to play that harmonica, something amazing might happen."

"Like what?" Daniel asked.

"Sadly, I don't know. I never played long enough to find out. But I've always heard that there's something magical about the gift of a harmonica. So promise me, Daniel, that you'll tell me if you find out what it is."

Daniel played his harmonica as often as he could. Soon, he could play clear, single notes and beautifully harmonized chords. He learned to play songs like "A Bicycle Built for Two" and "The Streets of Laredo." His parents were always delighted with his nightly concerts. And every time he played, Daniel was reminded of his grandfather's words. He waited and hoped for something amazing to happen.

One Saturday morning, Daniel's father had some business in town and he took his son with him. Daniel sat in the front seat and played "She'll Be Comin' 'Round the Mountain" while his dad sang along. They stopped in front of Watson Park.

"I have to go into the bank around the corner. It might take awhile," his father said. "You can come with me or sit across the street in the park."

"I'll stay in the park and play my harp."

"OK. And maybe we'll get some ice cream on the way home," his father said.

Daniel sat playing his harmonica softly and slowly while people passed by. As he began a second verse of "Oh Susanna," he was surprised to hear the sound of another harmonica. A teenage boy with a silver harmonica just like Daniel's was walking toward him. He stopped, smiled, and encouraged Daniel to keep playing. They shared several verses together. Daniel was wide-eyed watching the teenage boy slide incredibly fast up and down the harmonica.

Soon an older gentleman in a brown suit coat and gray cap joined Daniel and the teenage boy. He stomped his feet and sang along with his harmonica playing.

By this time, a small crowd was gathering. A young, pretty woman stepped forward and sat down next to Daniel. She pulled a harmonica from her green purse and played along to "My Darling Clementine." She created the most astonishing "wah-wah" sounds by fluttering her hands around her harmonica.

So there sat Daniel, with three strangers, now playing "When the Saints Go Marching In." Daniel tried to keep up with his very talented companions as they then began playing "America the Beautiful."

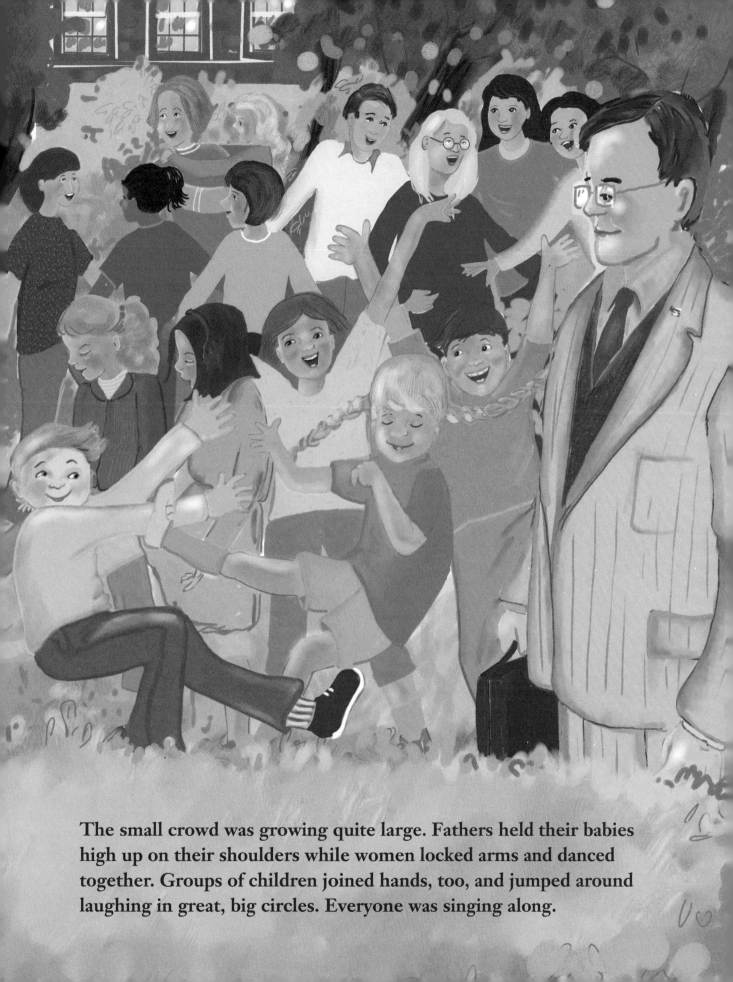

The small crowd was growing quite large. Fathers held their babies high up on their shoulders while women locked arms and danced together. Groups of children joined hands, too, and jumped around laughing in great, big circles. Everyone was singing along.

Mr. Crick, from Crick's Ice Cream Parlor, was in the crowd. He rushed back to his shop and returned moments later with dozens of chocolate, strawberry, and vanilla ice cream cones and gave them away to everyone in the park.

Mrs. Franklin, of Franklin's Toy Shop, loved the performance as she watched from her store window. She merrily marched across Main Street with red, blue, and green balloons for all the children.

Surprisingly, a big-top circus arrived in town.
The long, winding caravan slowed as it approached the
park. There were huge, smoky trucks with enormous,
steel cages containing wild beasts from faraway lands.

Hundreds of circus folk poured into Watson Park. There were clowns, sword swallowers, fire breathing men, and high-wire acrobats. A very thin man on tall wooden stilts strolled by with a woman juggling five flaming torches.

The wild beasts roared, trumpeted, and howled as if singing with the music. Clowns danced with each other and painted up people's faces.

Sword swallowers sang and swallowed their shiny blades. Fire breathing men spit flames towering above the crowd. The very thin man on tall wooden stilts skipped and hopped about in the street. The juggling woman threw her flaming torches high in the air while the high-wire acrobats tossed and turned each other even higher into the sky.

All traffic stopped as it came to Watson Park. The town square was one huge harmonica festival. Daniel could hardly play his harmonica with the wide smile now on his face.

Daniel, the teenage boy, the older gentleman, and the young woman accompanied the chorus of townspeople as "Home on the Range" was chosen as the final song.

"Oh give me a home, where the buffalo roam, where the deer and the antelope play." Everyone was arm-in-arm, swaying back and forth together. "Where seldom is heard," rose their voices, "a discouraging word."

And as they sang the final line, "and the skies are not cloudy all day," the townsfolk held the last note extra long in hopes that the song, the music, and maybe the magic of the moment would last forever. A wave of thundering applause swept over the four smiling musicians. They bowed, holding hands, as everyone cheered and whistled.

As quickly as it began, it all came to an end. The crowds broke off into clumps of happy, singing families. The last of the ice cream cones were licked up and the last of the bright balloons were carried away. The caravan of wild beasts, clowns, and other circus people snaked its way out of town. Traffic was moving again.

Daniel shook hands with his fellow
harmonica players and bid them farewell.

Daniel was by himself again, playing his harmonica softly and slowly while people passed by. He watched his father cross Main Street.

"Sorry it took so long," his father apologized.

"It's OK, dad."

"I hope you weren't too bored."

"No, I definitely wasn't," assured Daniel.

"So, how about that ice cream?"

That night, Daniel was still full of wonder about his day. As he drifted off to sleep, he could not wait to tell his grandfather about the magic that had come from his gift of the harmonica.

Author's Note

One of the most wonderful things about the harmonica is that you do not need to learn to read music in order to play it. You can have plenty of fun making beautiful music without ever knowing the name of one single note.

Here are the two things you need to know:

First, most harmonica music utilizes something called *harmonica tablature*. Tablature is nothing more than a numbering system (it's an easy alternative to standard musical notation). The holes on almost every harmonica are numbered. In the case of Daniel's harmonica, each hole is numbered 1 through 10. Each numbered hole represents a note. So by using harmonica tablature, you can play virtually any song. Look at the number in the harmonica tablature, find the numbered hole on the harmonica, and play it.

But there's one more thing. The harmonica is unique among instruments in that you can play a note blowing air out *and* drawing air in. And you can do this on the *same* hole. Arrows are usually used to show you what to do. An arrow pointing up (↑) means to blow air out. An arrow pointing down (↓) means to draw or suck air in. So for example, if you blow (↑) on hole number 4 *and* then draw (↓) on hole number 4, you are playing two different notes.

As you play the harp more, though, you will want to try to get a good, clear single note (rather than a *chord*, which is playing three or more notes at the same time). Getting a clear single note will help you better play the melodies of the songs that Daniel plays. You can do this by puckering your lips around one single hole. It will take some practice, but with time, you'll get it, just like Daniel.

There are many different kinds of harmonicas. In the story, Daniel plays a C harmonica (a harmonica *tuned* to the key of C). It's a typical beginner's harp, one that you can easily pick up for $10 – $15 at your local music store. If you ask for a C harp, they'll know what you're looking for.

Included on the following pages is the harmonica tablature for all the songs in Daniel's story. Be patient and practice each song slowly. The more you practice, the faster and better you will play.

And always remember what Daniel's grandfather shared with him on his birthday: "When you learn to play the harmonica, something amazing might happen."

Good luck!

Harmonica Tablature for Songs from "Daniel and the Harmonica"

America the Beautiful

↑   ↑ ↑↑ ↑ ↑ ↓ ↓   ↑ ↓↑ ↓ ↓ ↑

6 6 5 5 6 6 4 4   5 5 6 6 7 6

Oh beautiful for spacious skies, for amber waves of grain,

↑ ↑ ↑ ↑   ↑ ↑ ↓↓ ↓↑ ↓ ↑ ↓ ↓

6 6 5 5   6 6 4 4 8 7 8 8 6 8

For purple mountain majesties, above the fruited plain,

↑↑↑↓ ↑↑↑↓ ↑ ↓ ↓ ↓   ↑ ↑

6 8 8 8 7 7 7 7 7 8 7 6   6 7

America! America! God shed His grace on thee,

↑   ↑   ↓ ↓   ↑ ↑ ↑↑   ↑   ↓ ↑ ↑↓   ↑

7   7   6 6   7 7 6 6   6   6 7 6 8   7

And crown thy good with brotherhood, from sea to shining sea.

My Darling Clementine

↑   ↑   ↑   ↑   ↑   ↑   ↓   ↑   ↓

4   3   5   4   5   6   5   5   4

Oh my darlin', oh my darlin', oh my darlin', Clementine.

↓   ↑   ↓   ↑   ↓ ↑ ↑   ↑   ↓ ↑   ↓   ↓   ↑

4   5   5   5   4 5 4   5   4 3   3   4   4

You are lost and gone forever, dreadful sorry, Clementine.

A Bicycle Built for Two

↑ ↑   ↑ ↑ ↑   ↓   ↓   ↑   ↓ ↑   ↑

9 8   7 6 6   7   7   6 7   6

Daisy, Daisy, give me your answer, do.

↓   ↑   ↑ ↑ ↑ ↓ ↓ ↑   ↓   ↑ ↓

8   9   8 7 6 7 7 8   8   8

I'm half crazy, all for the love of you.

↑ ↓   ↑ ↓ ↑ ↑   ↓   ↑   ↓ ↑   ↑ ↓ ↑ ↓   ↑

8 9   8 8 9 8   8   7   8 8   7 6 7 6   6

It won't be a stylish marriage, I can't afford a carriage.

↑   ↑   ↑   ↓   ↑ ↑ ↓   ↑ ↓ ↑ ↑ ↑ ↓   ↑ ↑

6   7   8   8   7 8 8   8 9 9 8 7 8   6 7

But you'll look sweet on the seat of a bicycle built for two.

Home on the Range

↑ ↑   ↑ ↓ ↑   ↑   ↓ ↓↓ ↓ ↓

7 6   7 8 8   7   7 6 5 5 5

Oh give me a home, where the buffalo roam,

↑   ↓ ↑   ↑   ↑   ↑↓↑   ↓

5   5 6   4   4   4 3 4   4

Where the deer and the antelope play.

↑   ↑↑ ↓ ↑   ↑ ↓ ↓ ↓ ↓ ↓

3   3 4 4 5   7 7 6 5 5 5

Where seldom is heard, a discouraging word,

↓   ↓   ↑   ↓   ↑ ↓ ↑ ↓ ↑

5   5   5   4   4 3 4 4 4

And the skies are not cloudy all day.

Red River Valley

↑   ↑   ↑   ↓ ↑   ↓ ↑

3   4   5   4 5   4 4

From this valley they say you are going,

↑ ↑   ↑   ↑   ↑   ↑   ↓   ↑   ↓

3 4   5   4   5   6   5   5   4

We will miss your bright eyes and sweet smile,

↑   ↓ ↑   ↓ ↑ ↓ ↑   ↑ ↓

6   5 5   4 4 4 5 6 5

For they say you are taking the sunshine,

↑   ↑   ↓ ↑ ↓ ↑   ↓ ↑

3   3   3 4 4 5   4 4

That has brightened our pathways awhile.

I've Been Working on the Railroad

↑   ↑   ↑↑ ↑ ↓ ↑ ↑ ↓ ↓ ↑ ↓ ↑

7   6   7 6   7 8 8 7   9 9 7 8   8

I've been working on the railroad, all the live-long days,

↑   ↑   ↑↑ ↑ ↓ ↑ ↑   ↑↑ ↓   ↓   ↑↓

7   6   7 6   7 8 8 7   8 8   8   8   8 8

I've been working on the railroad, to pass the time away.

↓   ↓   ↓   ↓ ↑ ↓ ↑ ↑   ↓   ↓ ↑↑ ↓ ↓ ↑

8   8   8   8 8 8 7 6   9   9 7 7 8 8 8

Don't you hear the whistle blowing? Rise up early in the morn,

↓   ↓ ↑   ↓ ↑ ↓   ↑ ↑   ↑ ↑ ↓ ↑   ↓ ↑

6   7 7   7 7 6   6 7   7 8 9 8   8 7

Don't you hear the Captain shouting: "Oh Dinah blow your horn!"

When the Saints Go Marching In

↑   ↑   ↓   ↑   ↑ ↑   ↓ ↑

4   5   5   6   4 5   5 6

Oh when those saints, go marching in,

↑   ↑   ↓   ↑   ↑   ↑   ↑↓

4   5   5   6   5   4   5 4

Oh when those saints go marching in.

↑   ↓ ↑   ↑↑   ↓

5   4 4   5 6   5

Lord, I want to be in that number,

↑   ↓ ↑   ↑   ↑   ↓ ↑

5   5 6   5   4   4 4

When the saints go marching in.

Oh Susanna

↑   ↓   ↑   ↑   ↓ ↑ ↑ ↑   ↓   ↑   ↓ ↑   ↓

4   4   5   6   6 6 5 4   4   5   4 4   4

Well I come from Alabama with my banjo on my knee

↑   ↓   ↑ ↑   ↓ ↑ ↑   ↑ ↓   ↑   ↑   ↓   ↑

4   4   5 6   6 6 5   4 4   5   4   4   4

And I'm going to Louisiana, oh my true love for to see.

↓   ↓   ↓ ↑   ↑ ↑ ↓

5   6   6 6   5 4 4

Oh Susanna! Oh don't you cry for me.

↑   ↓   ↑   ↑   ↓ ↑ ↑   ↑ ↓   ↑   ↑   ↓   ↑

4   4   5   6   6 6 5   4 4   5   4   4   4

For I'm bound for Louisiana, oh my true love for to see.

The Streets of Laredo

↑ ↑   ↓   ↑   ↓ ↑ ↓ ↑

3 4   4   5   4 4 3 3

As I walked out in the streets of Laredo,

↑ ↑   ↓   ↑ ↓ ↑   ↓

3 4   4   5 4 4   4

As I walked out in Laredo one day,

↑   ↓ ↑   ↓ ↑ ↑ ↓   ↑   ↓   ↑   ↓ ↑

6   5 5   5 5 4   5   4   4   3 3

I spied a young cowboy all wrapped in white linen,

↑   ↑   ↓   ↑   ↓ ↑   ↓   ↑   ↑   ↓   ↑

3   4   4   5   4 5   5   5   4   4   4

All wrapped in white linen, and as cold as the clay.

She'll Be Comin' 'Round the Mountain

↑   ↓   ↑   ↓   ↑   ↑   ↑   ↑

6   6   7   6   6   5   6   7

She'll be comin' 'round the mountain when she comes,

↑   ↓   ↑   ↑   ↑   ↓   ↑   ↓

7   8   8   9   8   8   7   8

She'll be comin' 'round the mountain when she comes,

↑   ↓   ↑   ↓   ↑

9   9   8   8   7

She'll be comin' 'round the mountain

↑   ↓   ↓   ↑

7   6   8   7

She'll be comin' 'round the mountain

↑   ↑   ↓   ↑   ↓   ↑

6   8   8   7   7   7

She'll be comin' 'round the mountain when she comes.

Harmonica tablature sources:

Duncan, Phil. Mel Bay's Harmonica Method. Mel Bay Publications, Pacifica MO. 1981.
America the Beautiful

Gamse, Albert. The Best Harmonica Method-Yet!. Lewis Music Publishing Company, Inc. 1971.
A Bicycle Built for Two
I've Been Working on the Railroad

Gindick, Jon. Country and Blues Harmonica for the Musically Hopeless. Klutz Press, Palo Alto California. 1984.
Red River Valley
The Streets of Laredo
She'll Be Comin' 'Round the Mountain
Oh Susanna
My Darling Clementine
When the Saints Go Marching In

Harp, David. The Pocket Harmonica Songbook. Musical I. Press Inc, Montpelier, VT. 1993.
Home on the Range

Rob Dubreuil is a middle school science teacher living in New Hampshire. He likes to write stories, play the harmonica, and hang out with his wife and kids. This is his first book.

Please visit www.danielandtheharmonica.com for more information about the author, playing the harmonica, and other fun things.

Ginger Nielson is a full time Picture Book Artist who lives at the top of a hill near the edge of a forest in semi rural New Hampshire. Her work is a combination of traditional and digital painting. There is a magic wand on her desk (right next to her harmonica) and a dragon in her basement.

This is her first book for Stemmer House Publishers. You can view more illustrations on her website www.gingernielson.com